# FED UP!

# FED UP!

## A FEAST OF FRAZZLED FOODS

### Rex Barron

G. P. Putnam's Sons

**A**nxious **A**pples

# Cabbage Crying over Coleslaw

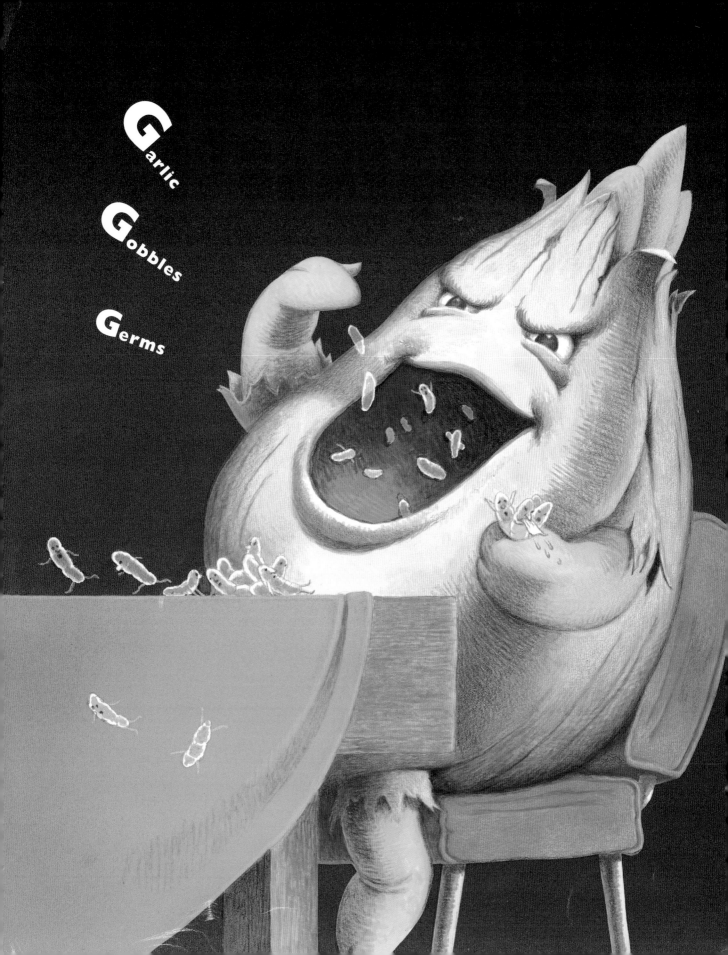

**G**arlic
**G**obbles
**G**erms

**H**ot **D**og **H**ates **H**ot Sauce

**I**mpatient **I**ce Cream

Junk Food

Gets

Judged

**K**issing **K**ohlrabi

Melon Melee

Nauseated Nectarine

# Potatoes Ponder Politics

**R**adishes **R**elax by a **R**adio

**S**uddenly

**S**alad

**T**omato in **T**rouble

**U**gli Fruit Needs **U**nderstanding

Vegetable Vaudeville

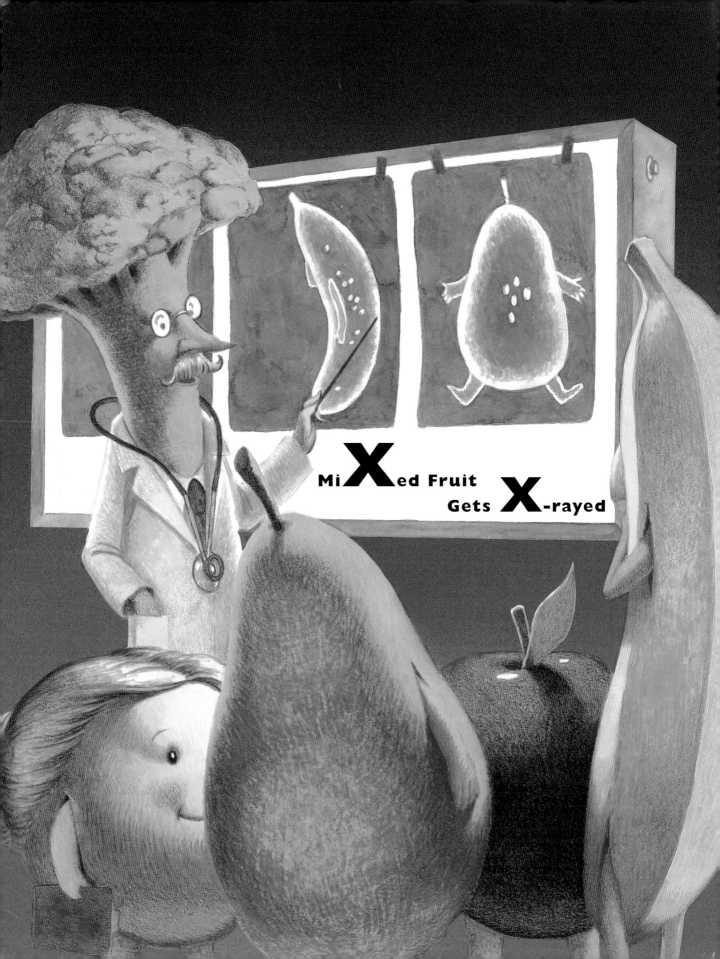

Mi**X**ed Fruit
Gets **X**-rayed

**Y**akking **Y**ams

**Z**en **Z**ucchini

to Alexander, Jennifer, and Kristen Barron

Text and illustrations copyright © 2000 by Rex Barron.
All rights reserved. This book, or parts thereof, may not be reproduced
in any form without permission in writing from the publisher,

**G. P. PUTNAM'S SONS**

a division of Penguin Putnam Books for Young Readers,
345 Hudson Street, New York, NY 10014.
G. P. Putnam's Sons, Reg. U.S. Pat. & Tm. Off. Published simultaneously in Canada.
Printed in Hong Kong by South China Printing Co. (1988) Ltd.
Designed by Semadar Megged. Text set in Gill Sans Extra Bold.
The art was created with acrylic wash and colored pencil.
Library of Congress Cataloging-in-Publication Data available upon request.
Barron, Rex.   Fed Up! A feast of frazzled foods / by Rex Barron.   p. cm.
Summary: In a series of alphabetically arranged scenes, a cabbage cries over coleslaw, eggs exit, oranges
object, and other foods are pictured to represent all the letters of the alphabet.
[1. Food—Fiction. 2. Alphabet.] I. Title.   PZ7.B275657 Fg 2000   [E]—dc21
00-023138   ISBN 0-399-23450-0
1 3 5 7 9 10 8 6 4 2
First Impression

## Did you know?

**T**omatoes, **E**ggplants, and **C**ucumbers are all technically fruits, but since
they are commonly known as vegetables, I have called them that on the **V**
page. I apologize to any fruits or vegetables that might take offense. **—R. B.**